D1360574

Hurray for Barbara Park
and the Junie B. Jones® books!

Laugh out loud with Junie B. Jones!

Check out Barbara Park's other great books, listed at the end of this book!

Junie B., First Grader®
Shipwrecked

illustrated by

Denise Brunkus

A STEPPING STONE BOOK™

Random House 🏠 New York

Copyright © 2004 by Barbara Park
Illustrations copyright © 2004 by Denise Brunkus

www.randomhouse.com/kids/junieb

Educators and librarians, for a variety of teaching tools, visit us at
www.randomhouse.com/teachers

Library of Congress Cataloging-in-Publication Data
Park, Barbara.
Junie B., first grader : shipwrecked / by Barbara Park ;
illustrated by Denise Brunkus.
   p. cm. (Junie B. Jones series ; #23)
SUMMARY: Junie B.'s journal entries start with Room One's stomach virus
excitement, the first-grade Columbus Day play, and getting the part of the
Pinta, the fastest ship.
ISBN 978-0-375-82804-1 (trade)
ISBN 978-0-375-92804-8 (lib. bdg.)
ISBN 978-0-375-82805-8 (pbk.)
[1. Sick—Fiction. 2. Theater—Fiction. 3. Schools—Fiction.
4. Columbus Day—Fiction. 5. Diaries—Fiction.] I. Brunkus, Denise, ill.
II. Title. III. Series: Park, Barbara. Junie B. Jones series ; 23.
PZ7.P2197Jsk 2004 [Fic]—dc22 2003018361

Printed in the United States of America 22 21 20 19 18 17 16 15 14 13

Contents

1

■ ■ ■ ■ ■ ■ ■ ■ ■ ■

Breathing Germs

Friday

Dear first-grade journal,

Today is the end of the week.

Mr. Scary is taking attendance. Attendance is the school word for who isn't here today.

There are lots of children out sick in Room One.

I am going to count them, I think.

I will be back in a minute.

Okay. Here is a teensy problem
I just ran into.
   'Cause how can I count the
people who aren't here? On
account of they didn't show up,
apparently.
                                harder
   Taking attendance is ~~dificulter~~
than it looks.
            From,
            Junie B., First Grader

I put down my pencil to think about this
situation.

   Only I didn't even have time to concentrate, hardly. 'Cause, all of a sudden, there was a noise on the other side of the room.

I turned my head to look.

And *SPLAT-O!*

A boy named Roger throwed up on the floor!

It was the disgustingest thing I ever saw. Also, the air did not smell delightful.

I quick held my nose and closed my eyes.

Only too bad for me. 'Cause my dumb-bunny eyes have a brain of their own. And they kept on sneaking peeks of the splat-o.

It was Cheerios, I believe.

Finally, I put my head on my desk. And I covered up with my arms.

Only just then, more trouble happened.

And it's called, a boy named Sheldon couldn't stand the splat-o.

And so he jumped up from his chair!

And he ran straight out of Room One!

And that was a surprise, I tell you!

Mr. Scary ran after him.

He brought Sheldon back in a jiffy.

Then he quick called the school nurse, Mrs. Weller, on the phone. And he told her that we need her help right now.

"Hurry!" he said. *"Fast!"*

And so, Mrs. Weller zoomed to Room One as fast as a speedy rocket.

And then she hurried over to Roger. And she talked to him in a calmy voice. And she said everything is going to be okay.

Roger hanged his head real embarrassed.

I felt sorry for that guy.

Also, he was making me ill.

Finally, Mrs. Weller helped him get up from his chair. And she held his hand. And she took him to her office.

After that, Room One could not do any work. On account of how can you do work with splat-o on the floor?

Only hurray, hurray!

'Cause pretty soon, our janitor named Gus Vallony came rushing through the door.

I jumped right up when I saw him.

"Gus Vallony! It's me! It's me! It's Junie B. Jones!" I hollered out. "Roger threw up! Roger threw up!"

Gus Vallony winked at me.

Then he went straight to Roger's desk. And he took out his important janitor equipment. And he sprinkled powder all over the splat-o.

And wowie wow wow!

That stuff sweeped up like a miracle!

We could not believe our eyeballs.

"Whoa!" said my friend named Lennie.

"Sí . . . whoa!" said my other friend José. "That powder is like magic."

I sniffed the air. "Yes! It *is* like magic, José!" I said. "Plus now it smells lemony fresh in here!"

Other children sniffed, too.

"Mmm. It *does* smell lemony fresh," said a girl named Shirley. "I wish I had some of that stuff for my mother. She *loves* to clean up messes."

"Mine does, too," said my bestest friend named Herbert.

Then, all of a sudden, Herb springed out of his seat very excited.

"Wait! Hold it! My mother's birthday is on Sunday!" he said. "And so *that's* what I'll get her! I'll get her a tub of that magic powder! What's the name of it, Mr.

Vallony? Huh? What's it called? What's it called?"

Gus Vallony's face went kind of funny. He glanced his eyes at Mr. Scary, and then back at Herbert again.

Finally, he ran his fingers through his bald hair. And he said the name of it.

"*Vomit absorbent,*" he said kind of quiet. "It's called *vomit absorbent.*"

At first, Herbert just stood at his desk very frozen. He did not say any words.

Then, after a minute, he did a little shiver. And he sat back down.

"Maybe I'll just draw her a picture," he said.

Gus Vallony nodded.

Then he packed up his stuff. And he waved goodbye to Room One. And Mr. Scary walked him into the hall.

While he was gone, Sheldon put his lunch sack on his head.

As soon as Mr. Scary saw it, he tried to take it off.

But Sheldon held on tight.

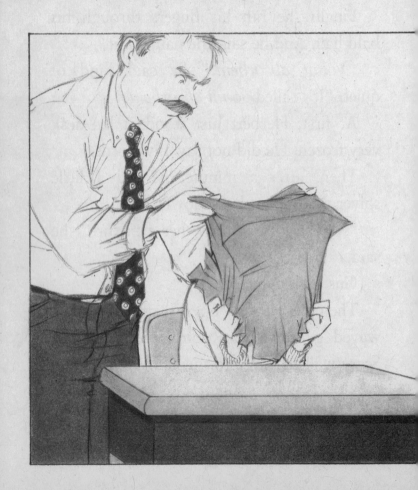

"No . . . don't! I need this!" he said. "If I stay in here, I won't catch Roger's germs."

I raised my eyebrows at that remark.

"Yeah, only I don't get it, Sheldon," I said. "How can you catch Roger's germs? 'Cause Gus Vallony just swept them up in his bucket, remember?"

Sheldon talked to me through his bag.

"Roger's germs aren't *just* in the bucket, Junie B.," he said. "Whenever somebody throws up, their germs shoot out in the air all over the place. Then, if somebody else breathes that same air, those germs can get sucked right up their nose nostrils."

I did a little cringe at that information.

Then I looked all around in the air.

And—very slow—I lifted my hand. And I closed my nose nostrils.

Room One watched me.

Then—one by one—they closed their nose nostrils, too.

And so all of us held our noses tight with our fingers.

And we didn't breathe for the whole rest of the morning.

2

Letting Go

It is not easy to hold your nose and eat a sandwich.

You cannot swallow good like that.

Also, you can't actually breathe.

The reason I know this is because Room One kept on holding our noses while we ate lunch.

My ears felt blocked when I chewed.

I tapped on my friend Herbert.

"I am not enjoying my cheese sandwich today," I said.

"Me too," said Herb. "I am not enjoying

my sandwich, too. Plus I don't even know what I'm eating. 'Cause I can't taste what's under my lettuce."

I thought for a minute.

Then I tapped on him again.

"Yeah, only what if you're eating something you hate?" I said.

Herb thought, too.

Then he quick put down his sandwich. And he lifted up the bread so both of us could see.

We leaned our heads in real close.

Lennie and José leaned their heads in, too.

"Hmm," said José. "This is only a guess . . . but I'm thinking tuna salad."

Lennie shook his head. "I'm thinking ham spread."

Herb made a face.

"I'm thinking I'm done," he said.

After that, he got out his apple. And he tried to take a bite. Only he couldn't actually get it in his mouth. On account of he was still holding his nostrils.

Finally, Herbert got frustration in him.

"I give up," he grouched.

Then he let go of his nose. And he breathed in a big sniff of air.

"Mmm . . . ahhh . . . air," he said.

It looked good to do that.

I let go of my nostrils and breathed, too.

"Mmm . . . ahhh . . . air," I said.

Next to me, May's whole mouth came open. She did the cuckoo sign at us.

"You two are *crazy* to do that," she said. "Dirty, nasty germs are getting sucked right up your nose this very minute, I bet."

I looked surprised at that news.

"Really, May?" I said. "Thank you for telling me that."

Then I leaned over next to her. And I breathed out my nose air on her shoulder.

"There. All gone," I said.

May did a gasp.

"EW! EW! EW!" she hollered real loud.

Then she jumped right up. And she tattle-taled to Mr. Scary at the front of the table.

"Mr. Scary! Mr. Scary! Junie Jones breathed nose air on my shoulder! And now I've got germs on me!" she yelled.

Mr. Scary kept on eating his lunch.

He was pretending May was not there, I believe.

May kept on tapping on his arm. And she wiped her shoulder.

"Nose air! Nose air! Nose air!" she hollered in his ear.

Finally, Mr. Scary stood up real calm. And he walked May back to her seat.

"Boys and girls, I know that many of you are still worried about what happened to Roger this morning," he said. "And I promise that we'll talk more about this after recess, okay? But right now, I want all of you to release your nostrils. And eat your lunch."

He stood there and waited.

One by one, all of us let go of our nostrils.

Only not Sheldon.

Instead, Sheldon ducked his head under the lunch table. And he said he was looking for his pickle.

I peeked at him under there.

He was hiding under his napkin holding his nose.

When the bell finally rang for recess, Room One was the first class out the door.

"FRESH AIR! FRESH AIR! FRESH AIR!" we shouted very joyful.

Then all of us breathed big snorts of breath. Because Roger couldn't have shot his germs all the way outside, probably.

After that, we skipped and jumped and clapped and played.

Except for not Sheldon.

And not May.

Sheldon sat down and held his nostrils some more.

May went to the water fountain and washed her shoulder.

3

V-I-R-U-S

It is still Friday.

Dear first-grade journal,

We just came in from recess.

We are waiting for Mrs.
Weller to talk to us about
germs.

May started holding her nose
again.

Also Sheldon put another
paper bag on his head.

> Today is an ~~intersting~~ interesting day in Room One.
>
> From,
>
> Junie B., First Grader

Just then, there was a knock at our door. And Mrs. Weller came in.

Mr. Scary went to meet her.

"Mrs. Weller, I'm very glad you could come back," he said. "Room One is still worried about what happened to Roger this morning. And we need some advice about how to stay healthy."

Mrs. Weller's eyes glanced over to Sheldon's bag head.

Mr. Scary's eyes glanced there, too.

"Some of us are a little more worried

than others," he said kind of soft.

Mrs. Weller went to the board. And she printed some big letters:

V-I-R-U-S

"Virus," she said. "These letters spell the word *virus,* children. Have any of you ever heard the word *virus* before?"

Lucille jumped right up.

"I have! I have!" she said real excited. "My nanna grows viruses all over the place! You should see our house, Nurse! Sometimes we have fresh viruses in every single room, almost!"

For a second, Mrs. Weller's face went funny. Then, all of a sudden, a light bulb came on in her head, I think.

"Ohhhhh. I think you mean *irises,* Lucille," she said. "Irises are very beautiful flowers, aren't they? But *viruses* are tiny little germs that can make people sick."

Lucille started fluffing her hair very embarrassed.

Then she fluffed and fluffed and fluffed.

Until finally, she sat down again.

Mrs. Weller kept on talking.

"Boys and girls, there's a stomach virus going around school. And I'm guessing that your classmate Roger has caught it now, too."

May nodded her head and pointed at herself.

"That's why I'm holding my nose," she said. "See me, Mrs. Weller? I'm being smart by not breathing the germy air."

Mrs. Weller looked kind of puzzled.

"Yes, but you're still *breathing*, May," she explained. "The air is simply going in your *mouth* instead of your *nose*."

May looked shocked at that comment.

Mrs. Weller smiled.

"I'm sorry, dear. But I'm afraid it just doesn't help to hold your nose," she said.

"In fact, one of the easiest ways to catch a virus is to touch your nose with germy hands."

May didn't move a muscle. She just kept on sitting there looking surprised.

Finally, I leaned over and tapped on her.

"I think that means you, nose squeezer," I said.

Lennie and Herbert laughed real loud.

They enjoy my humor.

After that, Mrs. Weller printed four rules on the board about how to stay healthy:

1. Do not share straws or glasses or forks or spoons!
2. Do not share food or drinks!
3. Keep your hands away from your mouth, eyes, and nose!
4. Wash your hands—OFTEN—with soap and water!

She put down the chalk and glanced over at Sheldon again.

"Oh, and I'm sorry to have to tell you this . . . but you can't really *hide* from germs, either," she said. "So—for those of you wearing paper bags on your heads—there are probably thousands of germs in there with you."

For a second, Sheldon sat as still as a statue.

Then, all of a sudden, he shouted real loud, "AAUUGGHH!" And he quick pulled off the bag!

Then he zoomed straight to the sink!

And he washed his hands and face with soap! Plus also, he washed his arms and his legs with a paper towel.

After that, he took off his shoes to wash his feet. But Mr. Scary said *no*.

"We're not doing a full-body scrub, son," he said. "Your face and hands are enough."

Sheldon looked upset.

"But germs can get on other places, too," he said. "Like what if someone drools on your arm? Or what if you get burped on? Or what if you fall down on top of a sick person, and he sneezes germs right directly up your nostrils?"

Mr. Scary rolled his eyes. "Come on, Sheldon. Now you're just being silly," he said. "I've been around a long time. And believe me, no one has *ever* sneezed germs directly up my nostrils."

After that, he took Sheldon's hand. And he sat him down again.

Pretty soon, Mrs. Weller had to go back to her office. But before she left, she took us to the sink. And she showed us the right way to wash our hands.

Room One lined up and washed very perfect.

Then we waved goodbye to Mrs. Weller. We were sad to see her go. 'Cause now we had to do schoolwork, probably.

Only here is what we didn't even *know*.

Mr. Scary had a happy announcement! And he'd been waiting all day to tell us!

"Boys and girls, I know we had a pretty rough morning. But I think I have some news that will cheer you up," he said.

He smiled. "In two weeks, our school is having an event called *Parents' Night*. Have any of you ever heard of Parents' Night before?"

Lennie quick raised his hand.

"I have!" he said. "My sister told me all about it. She said Parents' Night is the night when parents come to school and they poke their nose in your business."

Mr. Scary did a little frown.

"Yes, well, I don't really think that's the best way to put it, Lennie," he said. "Your parents don't come to poke their noses in your business. Parents are interested in what we do here in school. So sometimes they like to come to the classroom and—"

"Spy on us," said José.

"Butt in where they don't belong," said Shirley.

"Invade our own personal space," said Sheldon.

Mr. Scary closed his eyes a second.

Then he walked back to his desk real slow. And he sat down in his chair. And he ran his fingers through his tired hair.

"Okay. I'll get right to the point," he said. "This year for Parents' Night, I thought it would be fun to do something special. So I was wondering how you would feel about putting on a *play*."

My ears perked up at that word.

"A play?" I said kind of thrilled.

"A play?" said Herbert and Shirley.

"A play?" said May.

Then, all at once, Room One started clapping and clapping.

"A PLAY! A PLAY! A PLAY!" we shouted. "YAY! YAY! A PLAY!"

I springed out of my chair.

"I know a *lot* about plays, Mr. Scary!" I said. "On account of last summer I went to a real, actual children's theater. And I saw a play about a mouse. And that thing was a hoot, I tell you! And so maybe *we* can do a mouse play, too!"

Mr. Scary smiled. "Yes, well, I'm sure a mouse play would be fun, Junie B. But since it's October, our play is going to be about Christopher Columbus," he said. "We celebrate Columbus Day this month, remember? So Parents' Night will be perfect timing."

I thought it over a second.

Then I shook my head no.

"Nope, sorry. I think a mouse play is still the way to go here," I said.

Mr. Scary said *thank you* for my opinion and *please sit down*.

I tapped my foot kind of annoyed. Then I gazed my eyes around the room.

"Okay. Who would rather do a mouse play? Please raise your hands," I said.

Mr. Scary snapped his fingers at me.

Snapping means the conversation is over, I believe.

I sat down.

4

■ ■ ■ ■ ■ ■ ■ ■ ■ ■ ■

Finding Facts

That day when I got home from school, Mother was already back from work.

I like it when that happens.

She was in the kitchen with my dog named Tickle.

I gave her a paper Mr. Scary sent home about the play.

Her face smiled when she read it.

"Oh boy! Your class is going to do a play for Parents' Night, huh?" she said. "How fun!"

I shrugged my shoulders.

"Yeah, only it would be funner if it was a mouse play," I said. "But Mr. Scary says it has to be about dumb old Columbus Day."

Mother kept on reading.

"Oh, and look at *this*," she said. "It says that over the weekend you're supposed to look up facts about Columbus and his ships. And whoever has the most facts will get to choose their part first."

I rolled my eyes.

"Fact number one," I said. "Columbus is not a mouse. And so I don't even care about being in this dumb play."

After that, I turned around. And I clomped out of the kitchen kind of grumpy.

Tickle clomped with me.

We were almost to my room when my mother called after me.

"I just don't *get* it, Junie B.," she hollered. "I thought you always wanted to be a *star*!"

I stopped clomping.

Tickle stopped clomping, too.

"A *star*?" I said. "Whoa. I never even thought about *that* situation."

I quick turned around and zoomed back to the kitchen.

"A *star*?" I asked. "I could really be a star, do you think? Like the one and only star of the whole entire production, you mean?"

Mother grinned.

"Well . . . maybe not the one and *only* star," she said. "But still, if you bring in the most facts about Columbus, you'll be able to choose any part you want."

Just then, my legs jumped all around very excited.

"The *star* part, Mother!" I said. "I am going to choose the *star* part!"

I quick grabbed her hand.

"Let's go! Hurry! Hurry! We have to go to the library to get my facts straight!"

Mother undid my hand.

"Sorry, honey. But we can't go now," she said. "Ollie's right in the middle of his nap. And I don't have a babysitter."

I slumped my shoulders very glum.

"Darn it," I said. "Darn it, darn it, darn it. That dumb old baby ruins everything."

Mother wrinkled her eyebrows at me.

"Ollie's not dumb, Junie B.," she said. "And besides, you and I can go to the library tomorrow. Tomorrow will be plenty of time for you to collect your facts."

She stood there for a minute.

"*Or,*" she said, "if you want to do it right now . . . we can look up some Columbus facts on the computer. How does that sound?"

I grabbed her hand again and pulled her to her desk.

"Perfect!" I said real squealy. "That sounds perfect!"

And so me and Mother sat down at her desk. And she typed the name of *Christopher Columbus* on her computer.

And wowie wow wow!

A jillion pages came up about that guy! 'Cause he was famouser than I thought!

There were easy pages. And hard pages. And shortie pages. And longie pages. And picture pages. And poem pages. And there were even song pages!

Me and Mother read the pages out loud together. I read the easy pages. And she read the hard ones.

Then I wrote down lots of important facts we found out. And before I even knew it, I had *eighteen* whole facts printed on my paper!

I jumped down from my chair very thrilled.

"Eighteen! Eighteen! I have eighteen whole facts! And eighteen is more than my wildest dreams!" I said.

Then I hugged Mother real joyful.
And me and Tickle skipped to and fro.
And far and wide.
And round and round and round.

5

The Winner(s)!

Monday morning

Dear first-grade journal,

18 FACTS!

I GOT 18 FACTS!

I can't wait to choose my part in the play!

This is going to be the time of my life, I tell you!

From,

Junie B., First Grader

P.S. Two more kids are sick from school today. Plus Lennie just went to the nurse.

P.S. (again) Sheldon is wearing sandwich bags on his hands today. It is to keep germs off, I believe.

Just then, Mr. Scary finished taking attendance. And he said to please put our journals away.

"As you can see, we're missing three more classmates today," he said kind of frustrated. "It's going to be hard to do a play with so many people absent. But we'll keep our fingers crossed that our classmates will be back in time to participate."

Just then, we heard a rustly sound.

Sheldon was crossing his fingers inside his sandwich bags.

After he got done, he waved to Mr. Scary very pleasant.

Mr. Scary looked at him for a real long time. Then he waved back.

Finally, he stood up and walked to the board.

"Boys and girls, I thought it would be fun to base our play on the facts you gathered for homework," he said.

He picked up the chalk. "If you have a fact you'd like to share, raise your hand and I'll write it on the board. Then—when we've listed all our facts—we can choose our play parts," he said. "Now who would like to go first?"

José shot his hand in the air speedy fast.

"I would! I would! I have a *poem*!" he said.

Then he jumped right up, and he started to read.

In fourteen hundred ninety-two,
Columbus sailed the ocean blue.
He had three ships and left from Spain;
He sailed through sunshine, wind, and rain.

Mr. Scary smiled.

"Nice, José. That's a great poem you found," he said. "Let's see how many facts we can find there."

He wrote them down.

    1. Columbus was a sailor.
    2. He had three ships.
    3. He sailed from Spain.
    4. The year was 1492.

Just then, Sheldon started waving his plastic hands very urgent.

"I know the names of the ships! I know the names of the ships!" he called out. "They're the *Niña,* the *Pinta,* and the *Santa María.*"

"Excellent job, Sheldon," said Mr. Scary.

He printed the names on the board.

5. Niña, Pinta, Santa María

Then Mr. Scary started to call on someone else. But Sheldon stood up and read more from his paper.

"Columbus sailed across the Atlantic Ocean. He landed on some islands near America," he read.

Mr. Scary added the new facts to the list.

6. Sailed the Atlantic Ocean.

7. Arrived in islands near America.

"Okay. Well, thank you *again,* Sheldon,"

he said. "Now I think we should let some-one else have a—"

Sheldon interrupted. "My uncle Vern sailed to an island once," he said. "He came back with a woman named Bunny."

Sheldon kept on standing there. "Aunt Bunny has tattoos," he said.

After that, Mr. Scary hurried to Shel-don's desk. And he put him back in his chair.

May went next.

"My fact is about the *Mayflower*," she said. "The *Mayflower* is the ship that brought the Pilgrims to America. And so I am going to be the *Mayflower* in our Columbus play. Because both of our names start with *May*."

Mr. Scary looked curious at her. "Yes, but the *Mayflower* didn't sail to America until over a hundred years *after* Columbus," he said.

"I know it," she said. "But both of our names still start with *May*. Don't you *get* it?"

"Yes, May. I *get* it," said Mr. Scary. "But we can't change history. So I'm afraid the *Mayflower* won't be sailing in our Columbus play."

May sat down in a huff.

Lucille stood right up.

"My fact is about the richie queen of Spain," she said. "The richie queen of Spain was named Isabella. And she gave Chris the money for the trip. So I am going to be richie Queen Isabella in the play. Because if there's one thing I know, it's how to be rich."

José raised his hand.

"You shouldn't call him *Chris*, Lucille," he said. "In Spain, they called him *Cristóbal Colón*."

Lucille made squinty eyes at him.

"Chris . . . Crystal Ball . . . whatever," she said. "A queen can call you whatever she wants to."

She fluffed her hair and sat down.

That's when I springed up. And I waved my paper all around.

"Eighteen facts! I have eighteen facts!" I said real happy. "And so listen to this, people! The *Niña* was the *smallest* ship. And the *Pinta* was the *fastest* ship. And the *Santa María* was a big old tub."

Mr. Scary winked at me.

"Those are outstanding ship facts, Junie B.," said Mr. Scary. "Great job."

He printed them on the board.

And guess what?

After that, Shirley told him even *more* ship facts.

And so that's how the whole rest of the morning kept going.

Room One kept on telling him facts. And Mr. Scary kept on writing them down. Until finally, we'd told him every fact in the book!

Then ha! That's when the funnest part of all happened.

'Cause Mr. Scary walked around the room. And he counted how many facts each of us had listed on our papers.

And wait till you hear this!

He said, "We have a *tie*!"

Because me and my friend José *both* had EIGHTEEN FACTS!

We jumped out of our seats and gave each other a high five!

Then I skipped around my desk very joyful. Plus also, I skipped to the pencil sharpener and back.

Mr. Scary came back and shook our hands.

He said we would choose our play parts when we come back from lunch. And so meanwhile we should be thinking about what parts we want.

"Yeah, only I already *know* what part I want!" I said real thrilled. "And it is the bestest part I can think of. Only I'm going to keep it a secret till after lunch. And so nobody ask me. And I *mean* it."

After that, I pretended to lock my lips with a make-believe key.

Herb turned around. "You mean you're not even going to tell me?" he said kind of disappointed.

I got out my key and unlocked my lips.

"Okay . . . except for I will just tell Herb, and that's all," I said.

I locked my lips again.

José frowned at me.

I unlocked my lips one more time.

"Plus also, I will tell José. But that is my final offer. And I mean it."

Just then, Shirley did a big huffy.

"Okay, fine . . . and Shirley," I said.

That's when Sheldon raised his hand and pointed to himself.

Then all of the other children pointed to theirselves, too.

And so that day at lunch, I whispered my secret to everybody in Room One.

But that was all.

6

Teamwork

After we got back from recess, Mr. Scary went back to the board.

"Okay, everyone. It's time for the big event," he said. "We're going to begin choosing our play parts now. We'll start with Junie B. and José. Are you two ready to go?"

"Ready!" hollered José.

"Ready!" I hollered. "And guess what *else*, Mr. Scary? I'm even going to let José go first. 'Cause that will be very polite of me. Plus José already told me that he wants to be Columbus. And I don't. So being polite will work out beautifully this time."

I pointed at José.

"Okay, go," I said.

José looked annoyed at me. "But you already *told* him, Junie B. I want to be Columbus."

I clapped my hands real delighted.

"I knew it!" I said. "I knew being polite would work out good this time! On account of I want to be the *Pinta*! 'Cause the *Pinta* was the fastest ship! And the fastest ship is the winner ship. And the winner ship is the *star* ship!"

I skipped to the pencil sharpener and back again.

Mr. Scary said *please stop doing that*.

"Being the *Pinta* is fine, Junie B.," he said. "But you *do* understand that our ships will not be *racing,* right? All three of our ships will be arriving *together.*"

I did a little frown.

"Yeah, only that's not how I actually had it pictured in my head," I said. "'Cause a race will be more exciting, I think. And so maybe I will just arrive a *little bit* first. Like by an inch, or a foot . . . or half an hour, possibly."

Mr. Scary shook his head no.

"This play is not about stars or winners. It's about *teamwork,*" he said. "You are more than welcome to be the *Pinta,* Junie B. But you can't arrive before the other ships. Got it?"

I did a big sigh.

"Got it," I said kind of glum.

Mr. Scary wrote my name next to the *Pinta.*

Then he called on the other children to choose their play parts, too.

Lucille chose richie Queen Isabella.

And Camille and Chenille chose the Atlantic Ocean.

Then my bestest friend Herbert chose to be Land. And that is the importantest role of all, almost. 'Cause without Land, you can't actually land, probably.

After Herb, lots of other children picked their parts, too.

Then finally, it was May's turn.

May had to go last because all her facts were about the dumb *Mayflower,* and not about Columbus.

She stood up very grouchy. "All the good roles are already taken. So I guess I'll have to be the tubby old *Santa María,*" she grumped.

Mr. Scary wrote her name on the board.

"The *Santa María* is an excellent choice, May," he said. "The *Santa María* was the biggest ship. And it carried Columbus, you know."

May sat up a little straighter.

"It *did*?" she said. "It really *did*? It carried Columbus? Nobody told me that before."

She reached over and tapped on me.

"I bet *you* didn't know that, either. Did you, Junie Jones? If you knew that, I bet *you'd* be the *Santa María*," she said.

I rolled my eyeballs at her.

"Of *course* I knew that, you silly-head May," I said. "The whole entire world knew that except for you, probably."

May looked disappointed.

She turned her head back around.

I waited for a second to make sure she wasn't looking.

Then I slumped down in my chair. And tapped my fingers very annoyed.

'Cause guess what?

I didn't know that.

7

Ship Building

Friday morning

Dear first-grade journal,

We have been working on our play for the whole entire week.

We already ~~alredy~~ wrote some of our words.

And ha!

I am going to say, Land! Land! We landed on Land!

Only bad news. On account of

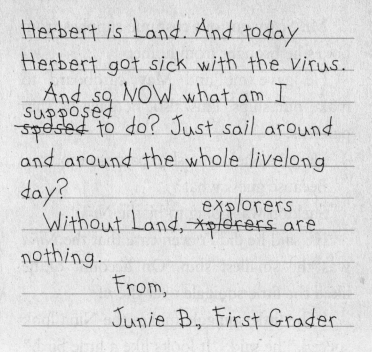

Herbert is Land. And today Herbert got sick with the virus.

And so NOW what am I supposed ~~sposed~~ to do? Just sail around and around the whole livelong day?

Without Land, explorers ~~xplorers~~ are nothing.

From,

Junie B., First Grader

Just then, the bell rang for school to start. And so I quick put away my journal. And I got ready to work on the play some more!

'Cause hurray, hurray!

Today we were making our costumes!

Mr. Scary got out costume supplies from boxes he brought from home.

He gave me and May cardboard to make our ships. Plus also, he gave us ship patterns!

He gave Sheldon a ship pattern, too.

Because guess what?

Sheldon was going to be the *Niña*!

He said he didn't even care that the *Niña* was the smallest ship. On account of he liked the little squiggle over the *n*!

"The little squiggle makes the Niña look special," he said. "It looks like a little bird."

Mr. Scary smiled at that comment.

Then he told us how to tape our ship pieces together. Plus he showed us how to make banners and sails.

"I'm going to color my ship banner red. 'Cause red is my favorite color," I said.

May looked down her nose at me.

"I'm going to color *my* ship banner *gold*," she said. "'Cause gold means you're the golden best. And the *Santa María* had to be the best. Or else why would Columbus choose it?"

I tapped on my chin very thinking. Then I did a little grin.

"Maybe he liked big old tubs," I said.

After that, I laughed and laughed at my own joke.

I see nothing wrong with that.

Pretty soon, Mr. Scary went to help Lucille.

She was not working on her costume.

"My richie nanna is going to hire her sewing lady to make my costume," she said. "Plus she's also going to buy me a crown of fake jewels."

Mr. Scary said *no*. "We're *all* making our costumes in class, Lucille," he said. "It's part of the project."

After that, he got an encyclopedia from the shelf. And he found a picture of Queen Isabella.

Lucille did a loud screech.

"Eeeesh! She's not even *cute*!" she said. "And what is that ugly hat thing on her head? Look! It has ear flaps!"

Sheldon ran over to see the ugly hat thing.

"Maybe she just got back from snowboarding," he said.

Lucille started to cry.

Mr. Scary said to please calm down.

Then he brought her a fake velvet towel she could use for a robe. And he gave her gold glitter to make a paper crown.

Lucille stopped crying. "Glitter?" she said a little perkier. "I get to use glitter?"

After that, she got right to work on her golden crown.

A little glitter can turn your whole day around.

At the end of the afternoon, our costumes were almost done.

Mr. Scary let us go to the front of the room and show the other children what we made.

And what do you know?

Lucille's crown turned out very beautiful! She looked like a real alive queen in that thing.

Plus also, I liked Camille and Chenille's ocean costume. They cut roly-poly waves at the top of a long roll of blue paper. Then—when they held it near the floor—it looked like the real ocean, sort of.

Me and Sheldon and May went last.

We sailed to the front of the room in our ship costumes. And we introduced ourselves.

"I am the *Pinta*. And I'm the *fastest* ship," I told them.

"I am the *Santa María*. And I am the *biggest* ship," said May.

"I am the *Niña*. And I have a little bird on my *n*!" said Sheldon.

Then all of the children laughed and clapped. And me and Sheldon and May sailed back to our seats.

Only too bad for me. On account of May sailed way too speedy. And she got to her desk before I did.

She looked very smuggy at me.

"What took you so long?" she said. "Are you the poky little *Pinta*?"

Then she laughed and laughed at her own joke.

That is not good taste.

8

■ ■ ■ ■ ■ ■ ■ ■ ■ ■

Practicing

That weekend was the longest day of my life.

I kept on wanting to get back to school so I could work on the play some more!

That's how come on Monday morning, I ran to my desk as fast as I could. Only I couldn't even stay in my chair that good. 'Cause I had excitement in my seat, that's why!

Finally, the bell rang for school.

And then wowie wow wow!

Mr. Scary took us to the auditorium to

practice on a real, actual stage! And that is a dream come true!

My heart was thumping and pumping when I walked up the steps.

Then all of us sat down on the stage floor. And Mr. Scary got us started.

"Boys and girls, we're going to begin with the very first scene, where Queen Isabella meets Columbus," he said. "Lucille and José? Will you come here, please?"

José and Lucille hurried to the front. Then Mr. Scary stood them on separate sides of the stage. And they walked toward each other until they met in the middle.

They said their lines.

"Hello, sailor. My name is richie Queen Isabella," said Lucille.

José did a bow.

"Hola, Queen Isabella. My name is

Cristóbal Colón," he said. "I would like to look for a new trade route to China. Can I please have some money to sail the ocean blue?"

Lucille pretended to think for a second. Then she fluffed her fluffy hair. And she pulled fake money out of her purse.

"Okay. Here's some money," she said. "But please bring back the change."

Mr. Scary quick raised his hand and hollered, "Hold it!"

"I don't really remember the line about bringing back the change, Lucille," he said. "Is that something new you've added?"

Lucille nodded. "Yes. My nanna and I thought of it over the weekend," she explained. "Nanna says that rich people *always* ask for the change. Or else how do you think they got rich?"

Mr. Scary stared at Lucille a real long time.

Then finally, he said, "Let's move on." And he called for the actors in Scene Two.

Scene Two is where Columbus picks out the sailors for his trip.

All of the sailors ran speedy quick to the front of the stage.

Then José stood on a box in front of them. And he said his next line.

"Who would like to sail the ocean blue with me? Please call out your names," he said.

And so the sailors called out their names.

And guess what?

One was named Sinbad! And one was named Popeye! And another one was named Captain Hook!

I clapped my hands very happy.

"This play is turning out better than I thought!" I said.

After that, it was time for the three ships.

I quick grabbed Sheldon's hand. And I pulled him behind me to the front of the stage.

And what do you know?

I got there first!

And Sheldon got there second!

And May was last!

I skipped all around her very springy. And I sang a happy ship song.

It was to the tune of "The Farmer in the Dell."

> The *Pinta* got here first!
> The *Pinta* got here first!
> Hi-ho, the derry-o,
> The *Pinta* got here first!

Mr. Scary made a mad face.

"Junie B., that's enough," he said. "For the very last time . . . this is *not* a race."

May stuck her nose in my face.

"Yeah, Junie Jones. This is *not* a race," she said. "Not, not, not a race!"

Mr. Scary bent down between us.

"I'm talking to you, too, May," he said. "If you two can't get along, I'll find someone else to do your parts. Do you both understand?"

May kept looking at me.

"*I* understand. Do *you* understand, Junie Jones? Huh? Do you? Do you? Do you?"

Mr. Scary stood back up.

Then—very silent—he took May to the back of the stage. And he made her sit down.

I laughed and pointed and waved to her back there.

Then bad news.

I had to sit down, too.

9

Shipwrecked

Thursday

Dear first-grade journal,

TONIGHT IS PARENTS NIGHT!
TONIGHT IS PARENTS NIGHT!

And good news!

Roger came back to school today! Only now he has a little bit of a cold. Only who even cares?

'Cause YAY! He's going to be Land!

        practiced
   We ~~praktised~~ our play three
more times today.
   It went very good.
   Except for Sheldon doesn't
want to sail to germy Roger.
Plus May kept on hogging the
whole entire ocean blue.
              From,
         Junie B., First Grader

As soon as I finished writing, the bell rang
to go home.

I quick put away my journal. And I
skipped out of Room One very gleeful.

Only ha! That night, after I ate dinner,
Mother and Daddy drove me right back

there. And I skipped back in again!

And guess what?

There were parents snooping every-where!

They were snooping at our bulletin boards. And snooping in our desks. And they were even snooping in our test papers!

All of the children had tension in us.

'Cause every test can't be a gem, you know.

Then finally, Mr. Scary saved the day.

He clapped his loud hands together. And he said it was time for the play!

Then whew! All of us got relief on our faces. And we hurried to the auditorium as fast as we could go. And we quick put on our costumes.

I tapped on Sheldon very giggly.

"My stomach has flutterflies in it," I

said. "Does yours, Sheldon? Does your stomach have flutterflies in it?"

Just then, Roger sneezed real loud near Sheldon's ear.

Sheldon made a sick face. Then he quick held his nose nostrils again. And he whispered the word *germy boy*.

Pretty soon, Mr. Scary made the shush sign. Then he smiled at us in our costumes.

"Okay, people. It's *showtime*!" he whispered very excited.

He did a happy thumbs-up.

We did a happy thumbs-up back.

Then, very slow . . .

Mr. Scary opened the curtains . . .

And our Columbus play began!

Lucille and José walked to the middle of the stage.

"Hello, sailor. My name is richie Queen Isabella," said Lucille.

José did a bow.

"Hola, Queen Isabella. My name is Cristóbal Colón. I would like to look for a new trade route to China. Can I please have some money to sail the ocean blue?"

Lucille reached into her purse.

"Okay. Here's some money," she said. "But please bring back the change."

After that, José bowed to Lucille again. And Lucille curtsied to José. And they walked off the stage.

The sailors hurried to their places.

My heart pounded and pounded inside me. On account of after the sailors came . . . *the ships!*

Mr. Scary lined us up to go onstage.

"Good luck, you three!" he whispered.

THEN WOWIE WOW WOW!
IT WAS TIME!
I swallowed very hard.
Then me and May and Sheldon sailed

right onto the stage. And we started to say our lines.

"I am the *Pinta*. And I am the *fastest* ship," I said.

"I am the *Santa María*. And I'm the *biggest* ship," said May.

Then Sheldon started to say his line, too. Only too bad for him. 'Cause just then, Roger did another loud sneeze. And you could hear it everywhere.

Sheldon scrunched his face very disgusted and looked back at him.

"I am the *Niña*. And Roger should wash his hands," he said.

Me and May looked surprised at that line. But Mr. Scary whispered to *keep on going*.

José walked out and said his next words.

"Ah! Three fine ships! Just what I need

to sail the ocean blue. Tomorrow we will begin our journey."

After that, Shirley walked out with a big sign. It said:

OKAY . . . NOW IT'S TOMORROW.

The audience did a chuckle. Only I don't know why.

Then Camille and Chenille stretched their ocean waves across the floor.

And hurray, hurray!

All of us ships began to sail to Roger!

There was a curvy line on the floor of the stage for us to follow.

We were supposed to sail side by side very perfect.

Only just as I thought!

Pretty soon, May tried to squeeze in front of me!

And that was just plain wrong. On

account of the *Santa María* was *not* the fastest ship. And you *can't change history*!

That is how come I had to speed up a teensy bit.

Only too bad for me.

Because when I speeded up, I accidentally nudged May's ship in her side.

And then *BAM!*

She nudged me back . . . *hard*. On purpose, I mean!

And *CRASH!*

The *Pinta* fell right off my shoulders! And I tripped over my ship! And I fell right smack on the floor!

Then OH NO! OH NO!

May tripped over my feet! And she fell down right on top of me!

And so Sheldon almost fell, too!

Only he quick did a swervy! And he crashed into Land instead!

And then *KABOOM!*

Both of *them* fell on the floor across from us!

And *that's* when the worstest thing of all happened!

Because, all of a sudden, *AH—AH—AH—CHOOOOO!*

Roger sneezed in Sheldon's face!

And it went *right directly up his nostrils*!

"AAUUGGHH!" yelled Sheldon.

Then he quick tried to get up. But he just kept falling down again.

And so Mr. Scary rushed onto the stage.

And he stood Sheldon up on his feet.

Only more bad news!

Because Sheldon pulled away from him.

And then *VAROOM!*

Fast as a race car, he sailed straight back to Spain!

And down the steps!

And off the stage!

And right out the auditorium door!

I did a gasp at that sight.

Then I sat there sickish and frozen. And May sat sickish and frozen, too.

'Cause now Columbus would *never* get to America.

And it was all our fault!

10

Surprise!!!

It was the terriblest moment of my life.

I looked at the side of the stage.

All of the children had shock in their faces. Plus Mr. Scary had shock in his face, too.

He quick hurried over to close the stage curtain.

Only that's when a miracle happened!

'Cause just at that exact same minute, José hollered, "WAIT!"

Then, zippedy fast . . .

He jumped right into the ocean . . .

AND CHRISTOPHER COLUMBUS SWAM TO AMERICA!

He did! He did! He *really* did!

He swam like the wind, I tell you!

And he landed right on Roger!

And all of the audience clapped and clapped!

Because Columbus got to America after all!

And that is not all the happy news, either!

'Cause the play was last night. And so today Mr. Scary brought a delicious cake to school! And we are going to have a *YAY, JOSÉ!* party!

Only there is still one teensy problem. On account of some of the children aren't actually speaking to me and May because of what happened in the play.

And so lucky for me that my bestest friend named Herbert got back from the virus today. 'Cause he already helped me write a 'pology to Room One.

I am going to read it after we have cake. On account of children are in better moods if they have sugar in them.

Here are the words I wrote to say:

Dear Room One (except for not actually May),

I am sorry I fell down at the play.

I am going to take all of the blame for what happened. 'Cause that will be big of me, I think. And so I am not going to ~~menshun~~ mention about how I got rammed in the side by another ship. Real hard, I mean. Like an iceberg.

Thank you for not being mad at me.

You are a delightful bunch.

Your friend,

Junie B., First Grader

P.S. In the next play, I will be a mouse. On account of ships can sink. But mice just float, usually. And so a mouse play is still the way to go, I think!

Ha!

Squeak!   Squeak!

Ha!

Don't miss these other great books by Barbara Park!

Rah! Rah! Rah!
Join the crowd.
Read these books
And laugh out loud!

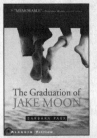

Hello, school children! Hello! Hello!
It's me . . . Junie B., First Grader!

I have been going to school for over one and a half entire years now. And I have learned a jillion things that will help you survive at that place.

And guess what?

NOW I AM GOING TO PASS THIS INFORMATION ON TO Y-O-U!!!

I wrote it all down in my brand-new book!

It is called: Junie B.'s Essential Survival Guide to School!

All of the tips and drawings are done by me, Junie B. Jones!

Plus also, there are stickers and pages for you to write in!

This thing is a hoot, I tell you!